BMX Racers

Dear Reader

When BMX racing became an Olympic sport for the first time in 2008, I was spellbound by the speed and skill of elite BMX racers from around the world.

I began researching BMX racers who came from New Zealand, my home country. I found out about some successful young competitors, Rebecca Petch and Sarah Walker, who both began BMX racing at a young age. Rebecca and Sarah were very humble about their extraordinary successes in top-level BMX racing, and that's one of the many reasons why they are featured in this book.

> SARAH AND REBECCA SHARED A STEELY DETERMINATION TO RACE HARD – OFTEN AGAINST THEIR BROTHERS!

It was inspiring and fun to meet Rebecca and Sarah, so I hope you enjoy reading their stories as much as I enjoyed writing about them.

Sharon Parsons

My sincere thanks to the following people for their time, information, images and enthusiasm for this book:

Rebecca Petch and her family, Te Awamutu, New Zealand

Sarah Walker, Cambridge, New Zealand

Ken Cools, Auckland, New Zealand.

NELSON
A Cengage Company

Contents

BMX Racers

1 What Is BMX Racing?

BMX racing is an action sport. People can compete in races around the world at various championship levels. Since 2008, BMX racing has been an Olympic sport. This allows experienced racers to compete at the highest possible level.

"BMX" is short for "bicycle motocross", and it describes extreme bike racing on dirt motocross tracks. "BMX" also refers to the style of bike used to compete on motocross tracks. These may have jumps, banked corners and various obstacles to challenge riders.

Speed, skill and safety are important in BMX racing.

A Snapshot of BMX Racing

1970s

In the 1970s, BMX racing began in the USA.

1980s

In 1982, the first of the BMX World Championships was held in the USA.

2000s

In 2008, BMX racing became an Olympic sport for the first time, in Beijing, China.

BMX Racing Tracks

BMX tracks are built outside and have varying designs and lengths – generally, they are about 400 metres long. The design includes straight sections of track between challenging jumps, small rollers and banked corners that test the riders' technique, skill, fitness and power. The banked corners help the riders to maintain good speeds. The dirt track can be covered with crushed lime "race rock" to give it a speedy finish.

building a BMX track

A BMX Race

A one-lap BMX race can last for 40 to 50 seconds, depending on the length and difficulty of the track. At the start of a competition track, there is space for up to eight riders to line up at the starting gate.

When the gate drops, the riders surge forward to race over jumps and around turns as quickly and as safely as possible.

A one-lap race that lasts for less than a minute puts pressure on the BMX racers to think quickly and skilfully – there's no room for mistakes.

A quick start is important.

TEXT TYPE
Information Report
PAGES 4–7

Riders have to be able to clear single, double or triple jumps that range in height from 6 to12 metres.

BMX Finish Line

As the fastest riders fly over the last jumps, their next automatic action is to pedal at even greater speed so they can lunge forward over the white finish line and try to finish first.

A Series of BMX Motos

To qualify for a BMX final, riders have to race in about three or four pre-final motos. The top eight BMX racers that finish with the least number of points in the motos earn a spot in the final. For example, a win earns one point, second place earns two points, and so on.

A Family Sport

BMX racing is a family-oriented action sport that can be enjoyed all year round by people of all ages and skill levels. As long as riders follow the race rules, wear the correct protective gear and ensure that their bikes are safe to ride, BMX racing can be a lot of fun.

SAFETY GEAR FOR BMX RACERS

2 Freestyle BMX

Freestyle BMX riding is also known as stunt riding. People get involved for fun as well as to compete. There are five main kinds of freestyle BMX riding.

Dirt Jumping: a BMX rider aims to gain as much speed as possible before riding over a dirt ramp and performing an amazing aerial stunt. The rider is judged on the stunt's originality, level of difficulty and the rider's landing.

Street Riding: in competitions, a BMX street course allows riders to perform stunts while riding up or down ramps and stairs, and along rails and the tops of walls.

Trail Riding: this involves riding a BMX over a series of dirt jumps along trails in places like the bush or forests.

Park Riding: many BMX freestyle riders ride in skate parks in their towns or cities, but in competitions they compete on special courses.

Vert Riding: BMX vert courses are designed for riders to perform stunts on a series of wide, long ramps in a supervised and safe place.

Rebecca Races BMX Bikes

Rebecca Petch lives in Te Awamutu, New Zealand, and since she was three years old she has raced BMX bikes in many competitions.

three-year-old Rebecca with her first trophy

Rebecca racing at four years old

Rebecca with the trophy she won as a four year old

Training Hard

For years, Rebecca has trained hard and raced hard against boys and girls to achieve her dream – to win as many BMX races as possible.

BMX nurtures newcomers

The race Rebecca won when she was four was reported in the local newspaper in 2002.

Before the Race

Rebecca has a pre-race routine. She says, "I usually ride a few laps around a practise track before a race, and then jump up and down quickly to warm up my legs and get focussed. When I go into the starting gate, Dad says, 'Good luck and go hard!'"

Rebecca focuses on the race.

"Go hard!"

During the 45-Second Race

"When I'm racing, I think about a lot of things, like what I'm doing now and which jump is coming up next and how to get there first. I also think about who is behind me and how to 'protect my line' so other riders can't overtake me."

After the Race

"All I want to do is take off my helmet, as it gets very hot. Mum and Dad rush over with a drink and we sit down and talk about the race."

Rebecca wearing her helmet

4 A BMX Racing Family

Rebecca's family enjoy watching BMX bike racing. Her father, Barry, raced BMX bikes for many years, but he became injured, so he stopped competing and started coaching Rebecca.

> "WHEN I WAS FOUR, I COULDN'T RIDE UP A VERY STEEP JUMP SO DAD HELPED ME."
>
> REBECCA

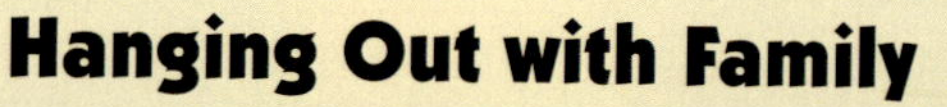

Rebecca (left) hangs out between motos with her cousin Josh (centre) and her brother Cameron (right).

Rebecca and Cameron at a BMX race day with their father, Barry

A Mother's Encouragement

Rebecca's mother Sonya says that Rebecca started out racing against boys, including her brother Cameron. "It has made Rebecca tougher to race with the boys and it has helped her in competitions, too."

> SHE'S AWESOME, REALLY COOL!
>
> REBECCA'S MOTHER

From left: Sonya, Cameron, Barry and Rebecca.

Rebecca's Pets

5 Training Hard and Fast

Rebecca competes in BMX competitions around New Zealand and in other countries, too. But in between races, she must spend hours each day training to improve her speed, strength, skill and race strategy. Rebecca also needs to be very organised because she has to fit in her homework and other sports, such as netball, touch football and basketball.

A Belly Crash

Rebecca remembers a training session when she crashed on a new double jump that was six metres high, and she broke a wheel. Rebecca said, "I fell flat on my stomach but I wanted to keep trying so Dad replaced my bike's broken wheel and eventually I did it!"

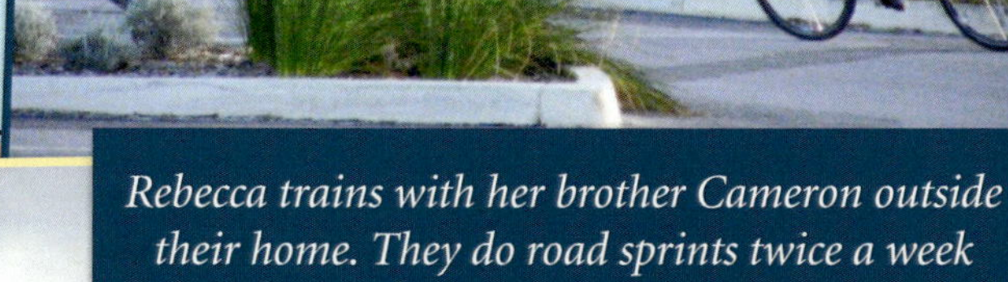

Rebecca trains with her brother Cameron outside their home. They do road sprints twice a week before school at 7.00 am for 15 minutes.

Rebecca trains with Cameron at the local BMX track.

practising jumps at the local BMX track

Going hard at the track!

A **Typical** Week for Rebecca

Monday: Race at the BMX club for two hours, including four 45-second races.

Tuesday: Train at the BMX track with her dad for two hours.

Wednesday: Rest day.

Thursday: Race at the BMX club for two hours, including four 45-second races.

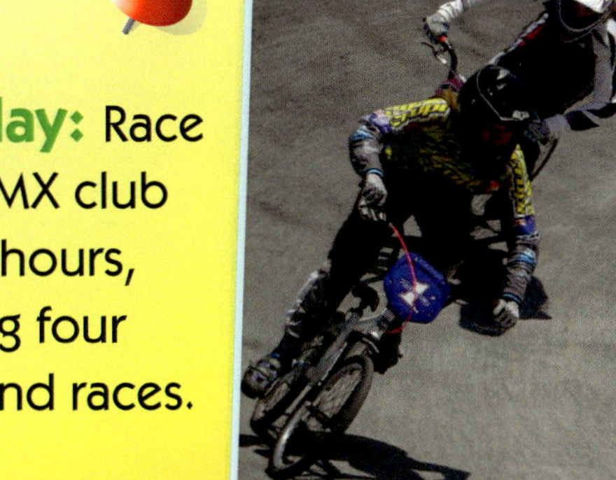

Friday: Rest day.

Saturday and Sunday: Travel to competitions around the country.

6 Trophies Galore

Rebecca has won many BMX championships around New Zealand and in other countries. Here are just some of her BMX racing trophies and bike plates.

Rebecca on her new BMX bike

Q: What are bike plates?

A: Bike plates are awarded to the BMX riders who achieve the top eight places in each championship. They can be fixed to the front of a bike.

Rebecca's bike plates (from left to right): World Championships Number Two, Oceania Continental Championship Number One, Mighty 11s Number One

some of Rebecca's BMX racing awards

WINNER!

"I'M PROUD OF MY ACHIEVEMENTS AND I HOPE I CAN KEEP RACING WELL."

REBECCA

SPORTS FEATURE

BMX Riders at the Starting Gate

A quick, clean start is important. All eight riders are lined up in their lanes with their front bike wheels resting against the low gate. They listen for a recorded voice to call out, "Riders ready!" All eyes are on the track ahead. When the riders see the red light, they pull their bikes toward their bodies and the orange light quickly follows. On the green light, the gate drops and the riders push down on the front pedal and burst forward.

7 World Number Two!

The Highest Prize

In 2009, Rebecca travelled to Adelaide, Australia, to compete in the 11-year-old girls category in her first BMX world championship. Rebecca won all her motos and finished second in the finals. Her finals result gave Rebecca the BMX title of "World Number Two" in her age group for girls!

Dual world BMX medallist

TC300709CT06

MOMENT TO CHERISH: Rebecca Petch, with her bike and trophies, back at Pekerau School with her proud teacher Nicky Vincent and classmates.

Pekerau Primary 'princess' Rebecca Petch won her silver medal the hard way at the World BMX Championships in Adelaide — coming through the toughest qualifying mottos imaginable in her age group.

The New Zealander was drawn in the same three 11 year girls' 20 inch bike class mottos as last year's World No.2 from Netherlands, the Australian No. 1 rider and a hot shot from Chile.

But reputations meant little to Rebecca.

She settled any nerves by destroying the field winning the first heat by two bike lengths.

A third behind the Netherlands and Chile riders in heat two was followed by another emphatic win by Rebecca in heat three.

The top 16 riders then rode off in two gates of eight in the semi-finals.

Rebecca notched up her third win in four races, taking out her semi-final from the Netherlands World No. 2, with Aucklander Zoe Fleming finishing third — both the Kiwis making the eight to contest the final race.

The difference between gold and silver came down to the first jump, which at 8.5 metres was uncharted territory for Rebecca, but which the European riders are familiar with.

The Netherlands team-mate of the World No. 2 established an early lead which the Kiwi very nearly chased down, at the same time fending off the challenge of the third placed American rider.

The Pekerau Primary student says she will never forget standing on the victory podium with her silver medal around her neck at her first Worlds.

Three days later she was pinching herself again standing on the podium a second time, sporting a bronze medal from finishing third in the 12 and under girls' cruiser class. The 11-year-old was only upstaged by two 12-year-old Australians in a field of 32.

On her return home, Rebecca was quick to acknowledge the role her Te Awamutu coaches, Malcolm McOnie and D[illegible] Hobbs had played in her stu[illegible]

"Malcolm has [illegible] I was three," she [illegible]

"Rhonda (Jan[illegible] Cambridge, and [illegible] club in general [illegible] heaps when I trained over there on Tuesday and Thursday after school."

The dual world medallist also acknowledged the sponsorship she had received from Te Awamutu's Cornerstone Trust, Magills Wholesale Meats and Electrics Ltd.

a newspaper article about Rebecca's achievements

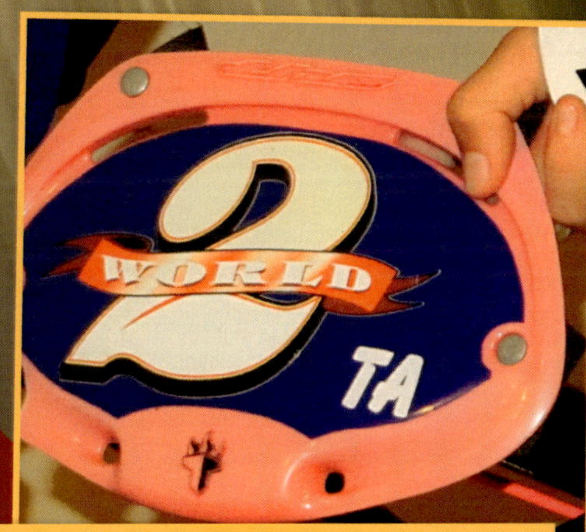

the "World Number Two" bike plate awarded to Rebecca at the 2009 World Championships in Adelaide

BMX RACING FEATURE

Rebecca Recounts Her First World Championship

We had been talking about it for a year, doing fundraising, organising flights, accommodation, all sorts of things, and of course training! It was finally here, Friday 17 July 2009, the day of our flight to Adelaide. The only bummer was that Mum and Cameron had to stay behind for a couple of extra days.

So off Dad and I drove to the Auckland airport at 1.30 in the morning. The Smiths followed us up there. Our flight was a bit late leaving Auckland, which meant we arrived in Melbourne late and then we had to rush to catch our flight to Adelaide.

Well, rushing didn't help!! We missed it and had to wait for four hours in Melbourne.

We finally got to Adelaide, got our hire car, found the motel and relaxed for a while.

On Saturday we all had to drive to the practise track. We were following the Smith family but then saw the Quintals and decided to follow them because we weren't sure where to go. Silly move that was. They stopped and told us they were lost!

Anyway we eventually got to the track and it was really windy like a tornado but that didn't stop the big boys from jumping the big jumps.

It's Sunday and I'm excited because Mum and Cameron are coming today! We went to pick her and Cameron up from the airport.

On Monday we went to the showground but we weren't allowed to see the track, so we got our armband, bike bands and number plates.

That day, Dad made sure my bikes – cruiser and BMX – were in tip-top condition ready for practise on Tuesday and Wednesday.

We got to the showground on Tuesday and saw the track for the first time. OMG what a cool track!! That ramp was huge, not to mention the first jump.

Thursday, the big race day had arrived, this is what I had been training for. I had butterflies in my tummy. Mum had packed my lunch in a bag, I put it over my shoulder, helmet on handlebars and said goodbye to Mum and Dad. They both said, "Good luck!"

In the pits, we were looked after by Rhonda, Sue, Laurel, Tony and some other friends. They were great.

When it was time for my race I went into the main part of the showground, up the ramps to the top to the starting gate. I coughed and up came the butterflies, now I was ready!

I heard the start call and I'm off down the ramp in my first ever world race. I couldn't believe it – I was in the lead and held them off right to the end. In the next race I got third place and I won the last heat.

It was really exciting. I had made it to the semis.

Then I came out and won the semifinal.

Finals time!!! We came down the ramp and darn it the Netherlands girl jumped the first, if only I could have jumped it, too. She was away but I wasn't giving up, I was chasing her hard with the American on my tail, we were battling for second and third place. I pumped as fast as I could and managed to stay in front of the American but still wanting to catch the Netherlands girl. But she was a bit too quick and I got second. World Number Two. WOW!!! I was blown away. It was so cool to stand on the podium.

I had another race day on Sunday on my cruiser. In my three qualifying heats there were seven Aussies and me, the only Kiwi! I got three first places. Go the Kiwi!

In the semifinals I got second place and in the final I was placed third. World Number Three (cruiser). It was an excellent feeling to be on the podium again.

What a cool week, but tomorrow it is time to pack up and go home to see my cat and dog.

Thanks for reading my story.

Rebecca Petch

8 A Mighty 11s Dream Comes True!

The Mighty 11s

The Mighty 11s is a BMX racing competition between New Zealand and Australia. Each year, five 11-year-olds compete to qualify for the New Zealand team, and across the Tasman Sea another team of five 11-year-olds have to race hard to represent Australia.

Rebecca lines up with her Mighty 11s team riders.

Rebecca Becomes a Mighty 11

In 2010, after the BMX World Championships, Rebecca was ready to try out for the Mighty 11s team. It was hard for Rebecca to qualify because there were a lot of competitors, but she did it!

Rebecca became New Zealand's first girl to be selected for the Mighty 11s BMX team.

a back view of Rebecca's Mighty 11 top

WINNER!

Rebecca Wins!

At the Mighty 11s competition in Casino, New South Wales, Australia, Rebecca was the only girl competing against her four other New Zealand team members and five Australian boys.

After five days of practise and racing in motos, Rebecca achieved her dream because she ended up being the overall Mighty 11s winner as well as the Mighty 11s top female rider.

Rebecca with the winner's Mighty 11s trophy

Magazine Write-Up

Young Te Awamutu girl creates NZ BMX history

OK, before we reveal to you the details of what was achieved by this Waikato 11 year old girl, let me give you some background information that will help you see the enormity of her recent achievement.

For over twenty years now and twice a year, both New Zealand and Australia have been contesting a trophy that is raced for by five of the best 11-year-old boys from each country: The Mighty 11 Challenge.

Some of the boys that have made the team in previous years have gone onto become professional BMX riders including our own Mark Willers and Kurt Pickard, along with Australians Sam Willoughby and Kamikaze, just to name a few.

This BMX trophy is steeped in tradition and when the Kiwi boys are representing their country they lay down the challenge to their Aussie counterparts by performing the Haka with vim and vigour, and the Aussies- well they just love it!

As an 11 year old you get two attempts to make the team. For the North Island titles, qualifying is held at the pre Norths, one month before the Labour Weekend race date, which is when the Australian boys come over to our shores. For the May exchange and the second in our race season, qualifying is done on the Friday before the end of year Nationals weekend, which is what BMX NZ have just held.

During qualifying the 11-year-old girls get to race with the boys, and over the years some girls have made it into the final but no one has managed to crack the big time and make the top five boys' team, and so it should be because boys are naturally stronger than girls.

Well that was until young Rebecca Petch stepped up to the mark this Easter weekend and not only made it into the boys' team, but did it in style finishing second overall out of the 50 or so boys who were vying for one of those five spots.

The current world number 2 and her family 'and supporters' were ecstatic at the result and cheered her on all the way, and didn't she look good with her aggressive 'take no prisoners' riding style! Petch won three motos out of four on the way to the final.

"Racing with the boys is a lot more aggressive than the girls. They don't hold back- they're just out there to win too," said a determined Petch after racing.

"My goal before the nationals was always to make the boys' team rather than the girls' team. Since I was a little girl I wanted to be the first NZ girl to make the New Zealand Mighty 11s boys' team.'

"I'm currently World Number 2 in my age group so will be gunning for World Champion at the 2011 World Championships in Copenhagen, Denmark".

So, history was made at this year's national BMX championships, by a young 11-year-old Waikato girl who will go down in the history of the sport as the first Kiwi girl ever to represent New Zealand in the boys' Mighty 11 trans Tasman race series.

a magazine article about Rebecca's inclusion in the Mighty 11s

MIGHTY 11'S TEAM CAPTAIN KIERAN NGATI (CLOSEST) GOING HEAD TO HEAD WITH FUTURE TEAM MATE REBECCA PETCH AT THE RABOPLUS BMX NATIONAL CHAMPIONSHIPS 2010,

History

Australia's Mighty 11s Team

In 2010, the Australian Mighty 11s team consisted of five boys – two from Queensland and three from New South Wales. Usually boys qualify for the team because there are many more boys than girls who try out, but in the year 2000, Melissa Mankowski became the first Australian girl to qualify for the Mighty 11s team.

BMX National Championship Win

BMX Sportswoman of the **Year**

At the 2011 National Championships in New Zealand, Rebecca won seven out of seven races, so she held on to her National BMX title for the fifth consecutive year. Rebecca was also awarded the *Sportswoman of the Year* trophy and *Top Female Achiever* trophy for being the first girl in 22 years to make the Mighty 11s team.

WINNER!

Rebecca races strongly at the National BMX Championships.

Meeting **Sarah Walker**

When Rebecca was ten years old she met her BMX racing idol, Sarah Walker. Just like Sarah, she wants to compete at an Olympic Games, too.

A first meeting!

The National Championships

In 2011, Rebecca and Sarah Walker competed at the National Championships in Auckland, New Zealand. They were both successful in their races.

Sarah and Rebecca at the National BMX Championships in 2011

10 Sarah Walker

Sarah Walker is New Zealand's most successful female BMX racer. In June 2009, in Adelaide, Australia, Sarah became dual World Champion for Elite Women and Elite Women Cruiser BMX rider at the age of twenty.

Where Did it All Start?

When Sarah was ten years old she began BMX racing because she was tired of watching her brother have all the fun on his BMX bike. Since then, Sarah has competed in more than 15 countries and won many championship titles.

Sarah has had a professional BMX racing career since the age of 17, and relies on sponsorship to enable her to race full-time all around the world.

> WHEN I NO LONGER ENJOY BMX RACING, I'LL STOP.
>
> SARAH WALKER

Sarah at the Olympics

Sarah competed in the BMX racing events at the 2008 Olympic Games in Beijing, China. Although she was disappointed with her fourth placing, she felt determined to win a medal at the next Olympic Games in London, England, in 2012.

Sarah's Preparation for the 2012 Olympics

Sarah needs to spend most of the year travelling around the world to gain as much experience as possible, so that she is well prepared to compete internationally.

A Typical Racing Year

Sarah travels around the world for most of the year. She says, “I would love more New Zealand girls to compete internationally, but I get used to travelling alone.”

JANUARY	FEBRUARY	MARCH	APRIL
New Zealand	New Zealand	New Zealand	South Africa
MAY	**JUNE**	**JULY**	**AUGUST**
the Netherlands	the Netherlands	Denmark	UK
SEPTEMBER	**OCTOBER**	**NOVEMBER**	**DECEMBER**
USA	USA	New Zealand	New Zealand

Sarah unpacks her bike after returning home to New Zealand from South Africa.

A Cool BMX Coach

Sarah’s coach is Ken Cools. A successful BMX rider himself, Ken was appointed by BikeNZ to coach Sarah and other New Zealand BMX racers for the 2008 Olympic Games. Ken and his family moved from Toronto, Canada, to live in Auckland, New Zealand. He says that a good BMX racer needs to work hard, be fit and skilful but also have dedication, passion and a desire to be the best in the world.

At the age of fourteen, Ken was the fastest BMX racer in Canada.

> “SARAH HAS AN INCREDIBLY NATURAL ABILITY TO RACE BMXS.
>
> KEN COOLS”

An Excerpt from Sarah's Travel Blog

6 May 2010, ITALY

Well, we got to Italy after a successful trip to Chula Vista – the US Supercross (SX) track and arrived to beautiful weather …

8 May 2010, ITALY

Time trials went pretty well. Marc Willers was the only one of the Kiwi guys to make it through …

10 May 2010, ITALY

Just a quick update tonight to say I won the time trials and came second in the final of racing …

15 June 2010, DENMARK

Arrived in Denmark on Monday to cold weather …

17 June 2010, USA

Spent most of the week at the Chula Vista SX track.

24 June 2010, USA

We (my coach Ken Cools, Trent Woodcock and me) started by flying from Los Angeles and drove down to San Diego to join the others, Marc Williers, Kurt James …

7 August 2010, SOUTH AFRICA

At Pietermaritzburg, South Africa. Well, the world champs are over for another year!

Racing finished this afternoon with quite a few good results from New Zealand. The challenge riders managed to pull off three world champs on day one.

24 September 2010, NEW ZEALAND

Heading over to Europe next week for the final round of the 2010 World Cup series in Frejus, France.

28 October 2010, DENMARK

Left New Zealand for the last international race of the season in the south of France. On the way, I detoured to Copenhagen, Denmark, for a few days of training on one of only three permanent Supercross BMX tracks in the world.

28 October 2010, FRANCE

Arrived for the final championship in Frejus, France.

11 Sarah's Accident at the World Cup

In 2009, Sarah Walker fell off her bike on race day at the World Cup in South Africa. Sarah recounts what happened.

"I was feeling good because I had qualified fastest. The accident happened while I was doing some final practise racing on race day. I was racing towards a very tall jump and I didn't have enough speed to break through the oncoming head wind and clear the jump safely. But it was too late to stop because of the momentum. So my bike stopped on the jump and I flew off the bike and landed hard on my side and hurt my braking hand.

"My coach took me to the first-aid area and I was told not to race. The first-aid tests showed that my thumb could be broken and they wanted me to have X-rays. I knew that I should play it safe and listen to their advice but I felt like I could still ride. Plus, after working so hard in training and getting into the qualifying rounds, I didn't want to miss my chance at the World Cup. So I did a deal: I said that I would go for X-rays after the race if they would strap my hand and allow me to race. My coach and the first-aid staff were not happy because they were worried I might do more damage, but I reassured them that I would be careful.

"After my hand was strapped, I deliberately carried my ten-kilogram bike with my sore hand to test its strength. My adrenaline was pumping as I carried my bike up the steps to the starting platform, which was eight metres above ground.

"I had three motos to complete before the final race. During the first moto, my hand was extremely sore and I raced cautiously. In the second moto, I went harder and I think the adrenaline helped me over the jumps. By the end of the third moto I had qualified with the fastest time. That really gave me confidence so in the final race I went really hard and ... I won the World Cup!"

Sarah's Second Accident

In New Zealand, Sarah's X-rays revealed no broken bones but her hand was still sore. Her injury was a mystery. Four weeks later, with a strapped hand and a small cast, Sarah travelled to the USA for another competition.

During the first practise lap, Sarah was following a group of US riders and they slowed down. But Sarah's braking hand was still sore and she couldn't brake in time. She swerved to the side of the track and lost control of her bike.

Sarah was suddenly out of the competition, and returned to New Zealand. The MRI showed that she had three fractures, which included a broken trapezoid.

MRI

"MRI" stands for "magnetic resonance imaging". An MRI is a powerful scanning machine used by medical professionals to take pictures of the body.

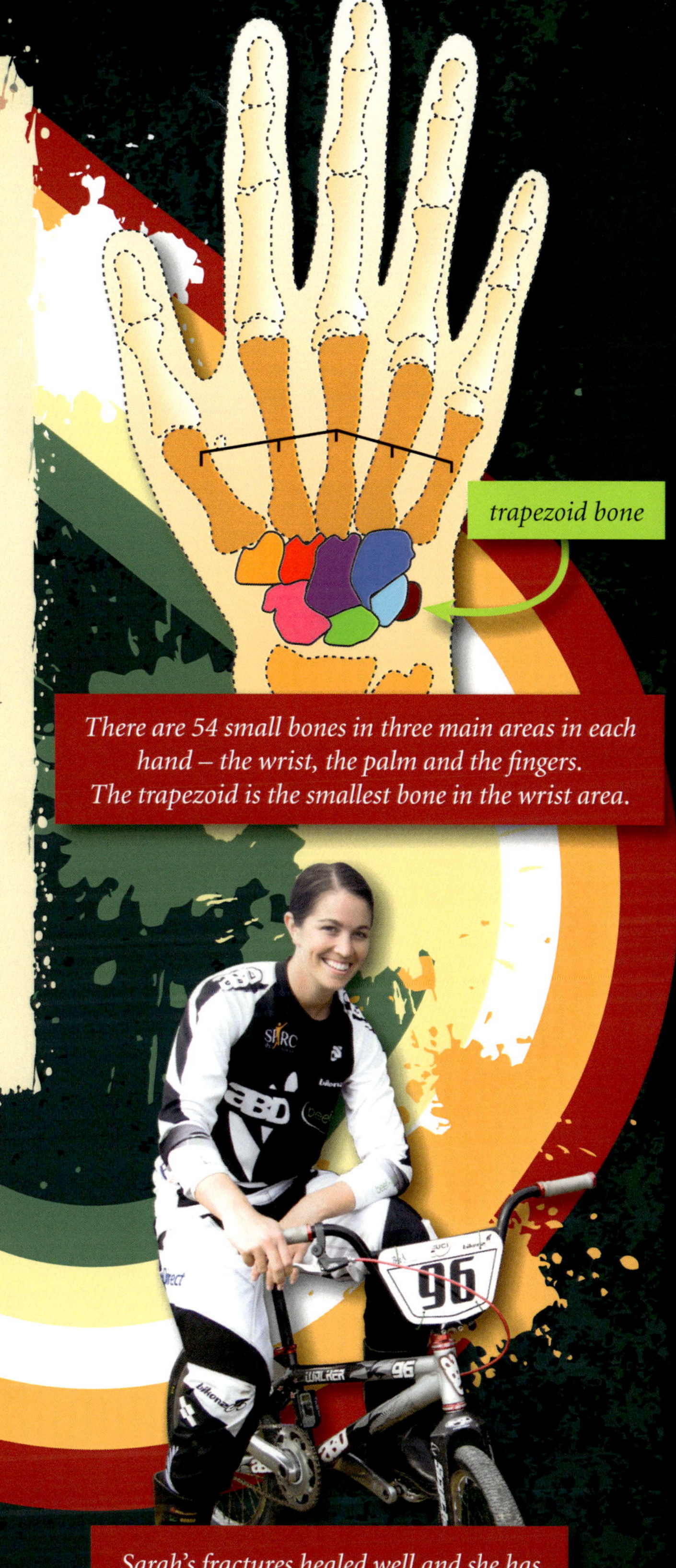

There are 54 small bones in three main areas in each hand – the wrist, the palm and the fingers. The trapezoid is the smallest bone in the wrist area.

Sarah's fractures healed well and she has continued to race successfully.

Index

Glossary

aerial Happening in the air

idol Someone who is loved and admired by fans

motocross A short distance motorcycle or bike race of at least two laps on a circuit with a variety of surfaces

qualify To show the required ability in a contest

sponsorship When a person or an organisation gives money to pay for an event or for someone's training

strategy A plan for achieving something

strength The power of your body and muscles

technique A particular method of doing something